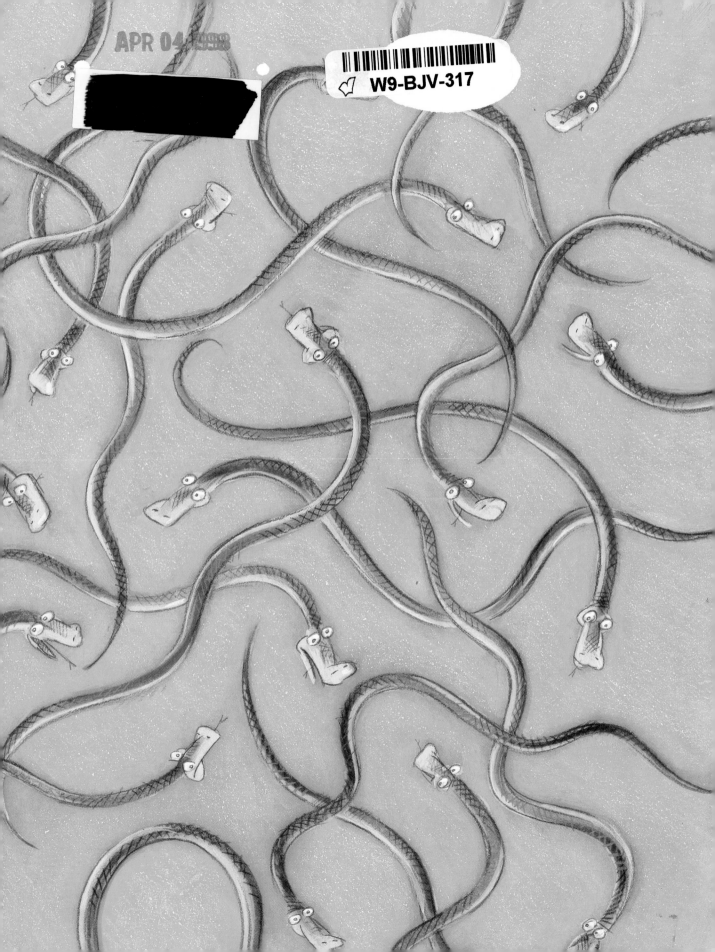

King Snake

WENDY SLOTBOOM

illustrated by JOHN MANDERS

Houghton Mifflin Company • Boston 1997

Text copyright © 1997 by Wendy Slotboom
Illustrations copyright © 1997 by John Manders

For information about this and other Houghton Mifflin
trade and reference books and multimedia products,
visit The Bookstore at Houghton Mifflin on the World Wide
Web at http://www.hmco.com/trade/.

The text of this book is set in 18 pt. Bookman ITC Light.
The illustrations are watercolor and colored pencil.

Library of Congress Cataloging-in-Publication Data

Slotboom, Wendy.
    King snake / Wendy Slotboom ; illustrated by John Manders.
    p.   cm.
    Summary: A talkative snake captures two mice, but his
verbosity helps them escape.
    ISBN 0-395-74680-9
    [1. Snakes — Fiction. 2. Mice — Fiction.]   I. Manders,
John, ill. II. Title.
PZ7.S6345Ki 1997   95-16370
[E]—dc20   CIP
                          AC

Manufactured in the United States of America

HOR 10 9 8 7 6 5 4 3 2 1

For Tom
—W.S.

For Patti and Paul
—J.M.

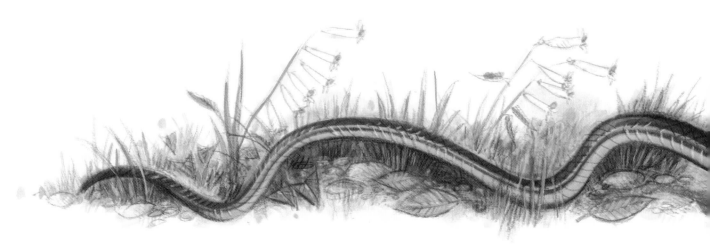

Henry and his best friend Tinkerton were taking the long way home when King Snake slipped around the bend.

As King Snake slithered to a stop, Henry and
Tinkerton ran to hide, but Tinkerton wasn't
quite fast enough. King Snake wound around
Tinkerton and held him tightly.

"Hello little mousie," King Snake said.
"H-hello," said Tinkerton.

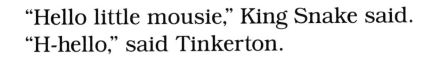

Henry ran back to help. He was smaller than Tinkerton, but he was also louder. "Let him go!"

King Snake smiled. "Let's talk."

"We can't talk to you," Henry said.
"My mother is expecting us."

"Oh, please," said King Snake. "I've just been talking to — conversing with — those swamp snakes down the road. My goodness, they are boring. What do they want to talk about? Just one thing, one thing only. Their swamp. It's disgusting, really. As for me . . ."

"What are we going to do now?" Henry whispered to Tinkerton.

"AS FOR ME," said King Snake. "As I was saying . . ."

"I'll try to think of a plan," Tinkerton whispered to Henry. Tinkerton was good at planning.

"AS I WAS SAYING, if you want to know the story of my life, if you want to know . . ."

"Henry," Tinkerton whispered, "keep him talking."

"Right," said Henry.

"PAY ATTENTION TO ME," King Snake ordered.

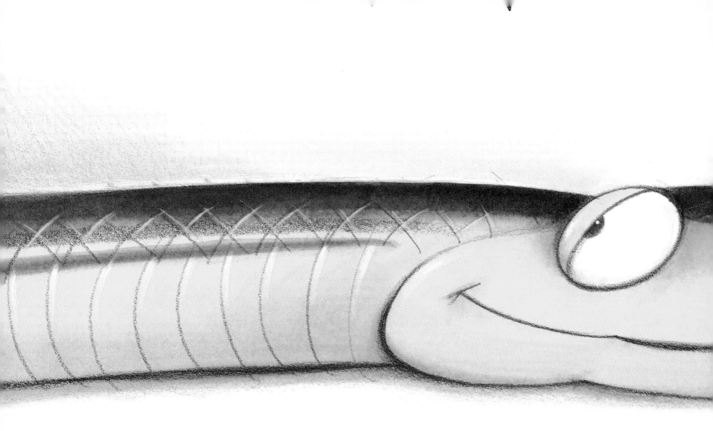

"If you want to know the truth, I am not a swamp snake or even a king snake," King Snake grinned, "I am a garter snake. Yes, it's true. I can see your surprise. I am named King Snake . . . just because I am. I like my name. KI-I-ING SNAKE. Ha-ha. That's me.

"A friend of a friend of mine once knew a sidewinder named Lefty. Lefty could wind only to the left, never to the right. Lefty went sidewinding to the left, to the left, to the left, right out of his home, the desert. Lefty was forced to spend his life in an awful meadow with butterflies and flowers. Ha-ha. Oh, don't feel sorry for Lefty. He was a real viper, if you know what I mean. All in all, I would not want to be named Lefty."

Finally Henry spoke up. "You should let us go. My mother will be looking for us, and I don't think you'd like her."

"Oh, I wouldn't? Why not? I really think — I truly believe — I would like your mother very much."

"She's a tailor," Henry said. "She makes
things out of, you know, snakes."

"No!"

"Yes . . . vests."

"That's awful, terrible!" said King Snake.
"But we won't think about that. Please
relax — I insist — and let me entertain you.
I have many stories to tell. I could tell
stories from now until . . ." King Snake
looked very sly, ". . . dinner."

"We have to be at my mother's shop before dinner," Henry said. "We have supplies to deliver."

"Supplies? What supplies? Something good, I'll bet. Something interesting. Show me right now."

"If I show you, will you let us go?" Henry asked.

"I don't know. I'll think about it. Oh, my indeed. I like to think about things." King Snake leaned toward Henry. "What's inside that sack?" he asked.

"Stuff," Henry said, and dumped it out.

"Well," said King Snake. "This is kind of boring stuff, if you don't mind my saying so, if I can be totally frank with you. I have seen better stuff in my life, if you know what I mean."

"This is good stuff," Henry insisted. "You can make things with it."

"Well, that's very interesting, I'm sure," King Snake said. "Like what, for instance, could you make? Give me an example. If you were to ask me, I'd have to say that fabric is boring, sewing is boring, and needles and thread and scissors are BORING, BORING, BORING."

Tinkerton stepped forward. "If you want . . .
Henry and I could make something right now."

"Yes," said King Snake. "Why don't you
make something right now, right this minute."

Tinkerton whispered his plan to Henry.

"What's all that whispering?" King Snake
demanded. "If you whisper to anyone you have
to whisper to everyone, and everyone means ME."

"I-I'm done now," Tinkerton said. He and Henry
began to sew.

"This is so cozy," said King Snake. "I wish Aunt Mathilda was here. She was always knitting us tubes to wear."

"I didn't know snakes could knit," Tinkerton said cautiously.

"A surprise?" King Snake said. "I like surprises, yes I do. I was surprised on my last birthday. What did I get? Nothing! That was a surprise all right. It was kind of sad, if you want to know the truth. It kind of made me cry."

"Where's my surprise?" said King Snake. "I can't wait. I'm turning — see, I'm turning. My surprise, where is it? I want it right now, right this instant. Why aren't you sewing? What have you done with your hats? You PROMISED me a surprise. I HATE TO BE DISAPPOINTED!"

King Snake slid close and nudged one of the mice. "You are no mousie! You are a furry winter hat." He looked at the other mouse. "So are you. Ha-ha! Ha-ha! Warm and cozy, warm and toasty, furry winter hats. Very nice, very nice. Surprise!"

"I'm going home now," said King Snake.
"I'm on my way. Here I go, I'm leaving.
So long, so long, so long. Good-bye, little
mousies. THANK YOU FOR THE HATS."

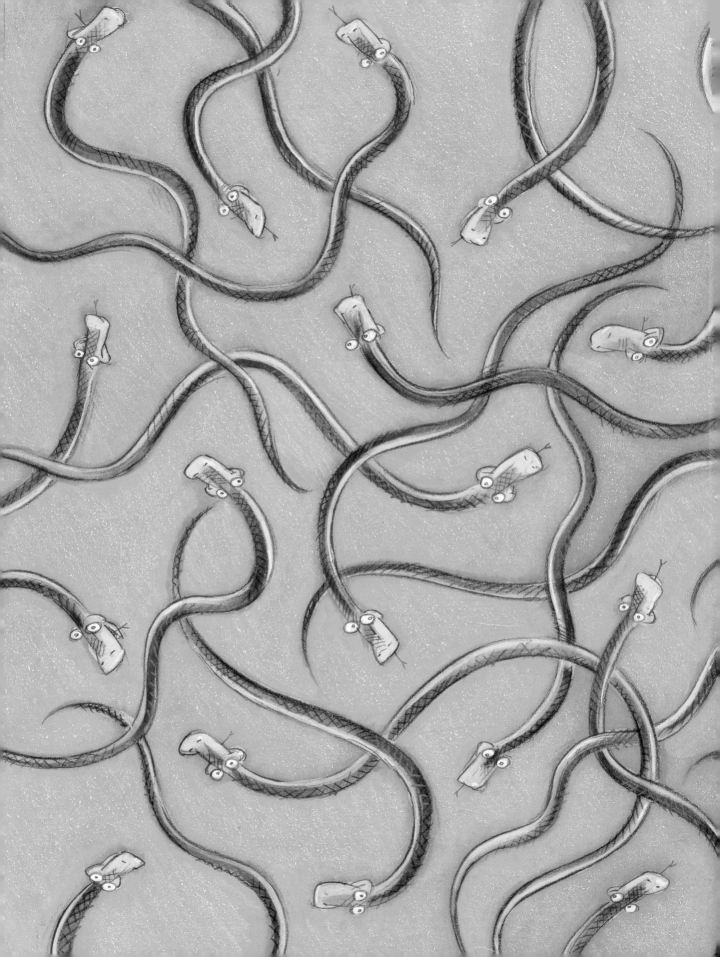